Sebastian Loth

Clementine

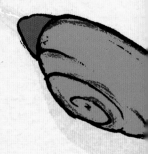

NorthSouth

NorthSouth
New York / London

Every evening a little snail sat on her favorite branch in the old clementine tree and stretched out her feelers into the warm breeze. The low autumn sun dipped everything in golden light and her small shell started to glow as orange as the ripe fruit beneath her, so the little snail was called Clementine.

Like many small snails, Clementine,
being round herself, loved everything round.

Even old car tires looked gorgeous to Clementine.
Her heart leaped with joy just to glide in a circle,
around and around and around.

Clementine was a happy little snail. But sometimes, on quiet nights when the bright round moon moved softly through the sky, she couldn't sleep. "So big," she thought. "So beautiful. So *round*."

Clementine longed to glide gently over the surface as the moon carried her tenderly around and around and around. And so she made a daring decision. "I'm going to fly to the moon," she whispered.

Clementine told her best friend, Paul, about her decision, and they got to work the very next evening. Together they planned. They plotted. They calculated. They diagrammed. Clementine was especially fond of Paul's compass—it let her draw such perfect circles.

"Yes, this could work!" exclaimed Paul.

They sawed and hammered far into the night.

Their first attempt was a trampoline they built themselves. But after her third jump, Clementine felt queasy. And one of her feelers was bent.

"Let's try something else," she said.

So they built something else. But the slingshot
only hurled Clementine into the bushes. And to
make matters worse, it started to rain.

Paul, however, found the rain inspirational.
As always when it rained, he had a brilliant idea.

A ROCKET!

"The world . . . it is . . . ROUND!"

she exclaimed
just before
she headed
back to Earth.

At the moment of takeoff, Clementine closed her eyes. She was actually a little bit frightened, but she was excited too. And suddenly there she was, rocketing into the night sky—higher, and higher, and higher. . . .

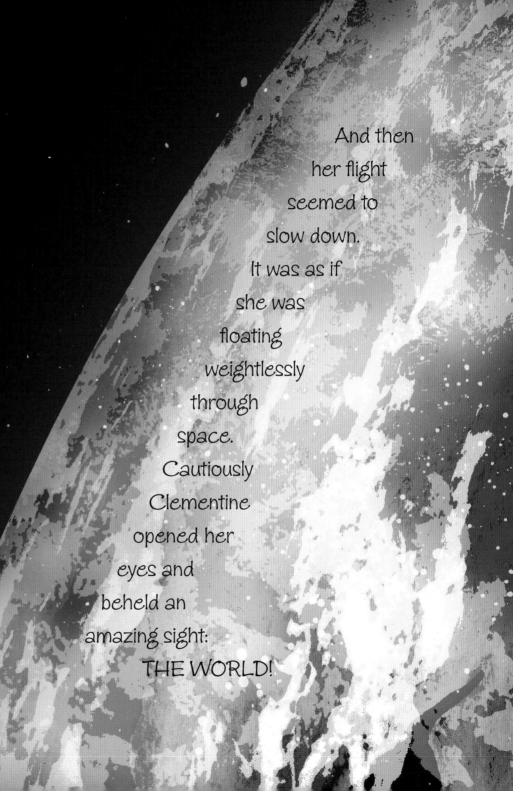

And then
her flight
seemed to
slow down.
It was as if
she was
floating
weightlessly
through
space.
Cautiously
Clementine
opened her
eyes and
beheld an
amazing sight:
THE WORLD!

Luckily Clementine landed squarely in the village pond without getting hurt at all. A bit of water got inside her shell, but it only gave her a little cold.

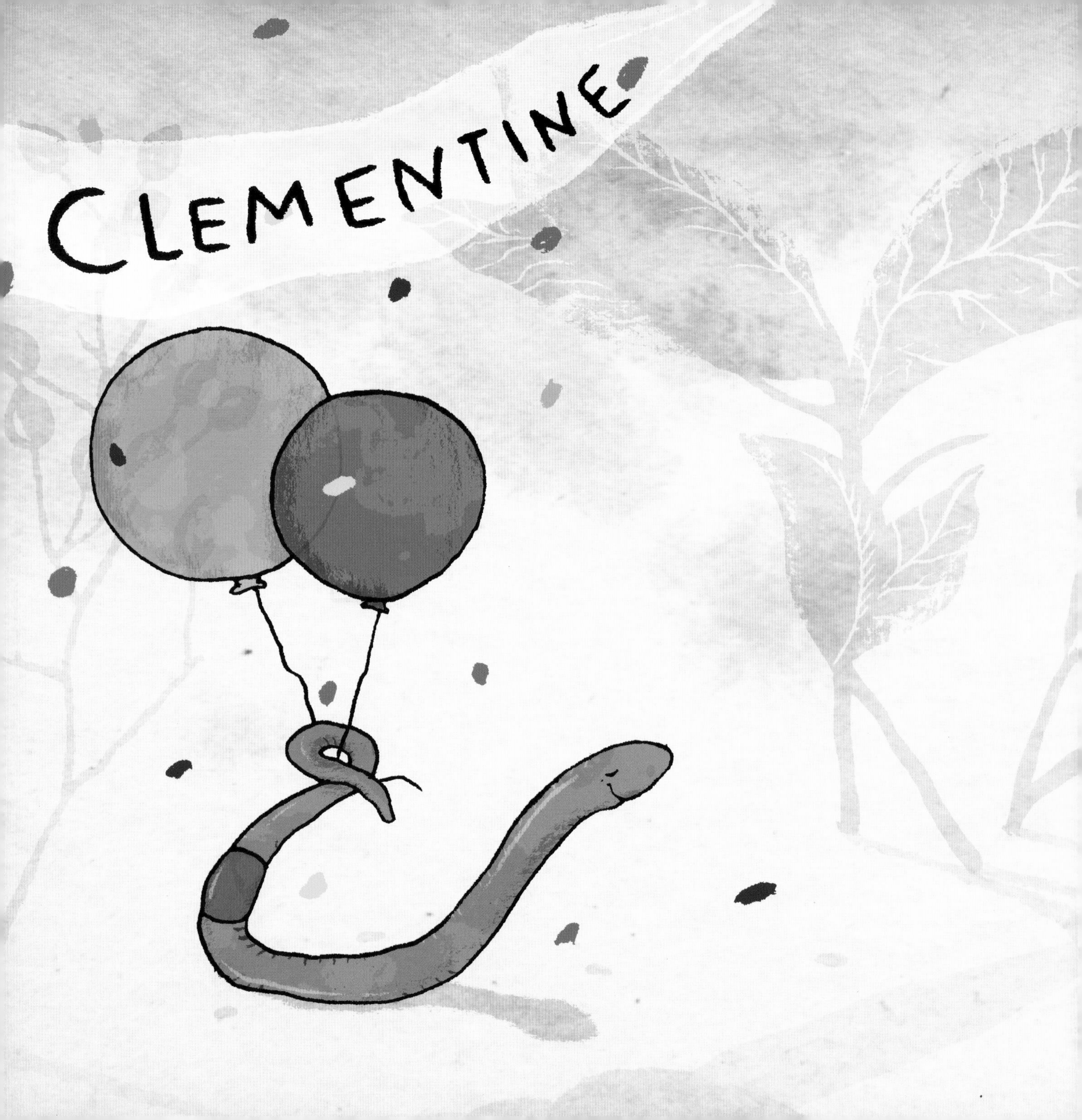
CLEMENTINE

Six weeks later, she finally made it home. Paul was there to greet her. Clementine was excited to tell him—and everyone—about her amazing adventure!

That night Clementine slept happily in the
bright silvery moonlight, dreaming of her great
discovery—that this beautiful planet she lived on
was ROUND—as the world carried her tenderly
around . . . and around . . . and around.

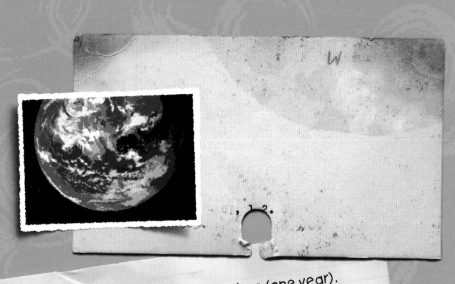

The Earth travels around the sun every 365 days (one year).

The moon travels around the Earth every 27.3 days (one month).

Almost ¾ of the Earth's surface is covered with water.

The Earth's land is divided into seven continents: North America,

South America, Europe, Asia, Africa, Australia, and Antarctica.

And, the Earth is ROUND!!!

Detected by